# THE BEAR

## An American Folk Song

## by Kenneth J. Spengler

MONDO

To Margaret, the girl in my life—K.S.

Special thanks to Kathy Boyd and Mark Gensman

Text copyright © 2002 by MONDO Publishing
Illustrations copyright © 2002 by Kenneth J. Spengler
under exclusive license to MONDO Publishing

For information contact:
MONDO Publishing
980 Avenue of the Americas
New York, NY 10018
Visit our web site at http://www.mondopub.com

Printed in China
02 03 04 05 06 07 HC 9 8 7 6 5 4 3 2
05 06 07 08 09 PB 9 8 7 6 5 4 3 2

First published in paperback in 2004.

ISBN 1-59034-190-2 (hardcover)      ISBN 1-59034-182-1 (pbk.)

Designed by Edward Miller

Library of Congress Cataloging-in-Publication Data

The Bear / illustrated by Spengler, Kenneth.
    p. cm.
    Summary: A young girl is chased up a tree by a bear and stuck there until she finds
help from an unusual source.
    ISBN 1-59034-190-2 -- ISBN 1-59034-182-1 (pbk.)
    [1. Bears--Fiction. 2. Stories in rhyme.] I. Kenneth Spengler, ill.

PZ8.3. B3753 2002
[E]--dc21                                                              2001054443

# THE BEAR

The other day,
I met a bear—
A way down there,
A great big bear!

The other day, I met a bear—
a way down there, a great big bear!

I looked at him.
He looked at me.
Oh! He was big!
I shouted, "Eeeee!"

*I looked at him. He looked at me.*

*Oh! He was big! I shouted, "Eeeee!"*

He said to me,
"Just run away!
I'll eat you up,
Right here today."

He said to me, "Just run away!

I'll eat you up, right here today."

And so I ran
Away from there—
And right behind
Me was that bear.

And so I ran away from there—

and right behind me was that bear.

The bear he growled
And nipped my heel,
And said, "You'll be
One tasty meal!"

*The bear he growled and nipped my heel,
and said, "You'll be one tasty meal!"*

Ahead of me
I saw a tree—
A great big tree.
Oh, golly gee!

*Ahead of me I saw a tree— a great big tree. Oh, golly gee!*

The lowest branch
Was ten feet up.
I had to jump
And trust my luck.

The lowest branch was ten feet up.

I had to jump and trust my luck.

And so I jumped
Into the air—
And missed that branch
A way up there.

*And so I jumped into the air—*

*and missed that branch a way up there.*

That mean old bear,
How he did grin!
He licked his lips
And wiped his chin.

*That mean old bear, how he did grin!*

*He licked his lips and wiped his chin.*

But don't you cry
And don't you frown.
I grabbed that branch
On my way down.

But don't you cry and don't you frown.

I grabbed that branch on my way down.

17

And there I swung
In that tall tree.
The bear just growled
Right up at me.

And there I swung in that tall tree.

The bear just growled right up at me.

And then I heard
A scary creak—
The branch above
Was getting weak!

*And then I heard a scary creak—*
*the branch above was getting weak!*

The branch would break,
And down I'd crash!
The bear would eat
Me in a flash.

The branch would break, and down I'd crash!

The bear would eat me in a flash.

"Ha, ha, ha, ha,"
Said that big bear.
"I'll get you now!
Come down from there!"

"Ha, ha, ha, ha," said that big bear.

"I'll get you now! Come down from there!"

What should I do?
I would not cry!
Maybe I could
Learn how to fly.

What should I do? I would not cry!

Maybe I could learn how to fly.

I yelled and yelled,
"Help! Someone, help!"
Then, down below,
That bear said, "Yelp!"

I yelled and yelled, "Help! Someone, help!"
Then, down below, that bear said, "Yelp!"

I saw his eyes
Grow wide with fear.
Could all this mean
That help was near?

I saw his eyes grow wide with fear.

Could all this mean that help was near?

25

I heard a *whooooosh!*
What did I see?
A giant bird—
And it saw me!

I heard a whooooosh! What did I see?

A giant bird—and it saw me!

It picked me up
And flew away.
Far down below,
The bear did stay.

It picked me up and flew away.

Far down below, the bear did stay.

Up to its nest
That bird did flap.
I was so glad.
I tried to clap!

Up to its nest that bird did flap.

I was so glad. I tried to clap!

"Now," said the bird,
"Don't be afraid!
Have pumpkin pie
And lemonade!"

"Now," said the bird, "don't be afraid!

Have pumpkin pie and lemonade!"

So here I am,
And here I'll stay—
Until that bear
Goes far away!

*So here I am, and here I'll stay—*

*until that bear goes far away.*

# THE BEAR

*Arranged by Frank Piazza*

1. The oth-er day (The oth-er day), I met a

bear (I met a bear), A way down there ( A way down

there), A great big bear (A great big bear). The oth-er

day I met a bear, a great big bear, a way down there.